A Knight To Remember

By

Charlie McArd

This book is dedicated to Charlotte Mcard "Don't Rush Me".

Also our grandson Oliver Mcard.

"Are we there yet daddy" said Charlotte who was in the back seat of the car playing with her iPad "Yes my little pumpkin we are not far now, do you know what I'm going to do when we get home I'm going to write a song called, Are We There Yet ha-ha" Charlottes dad Charlie was a budding singer songwriter who played in a local band around the north west of England called, The Mendips named after John Lennon's house in Liverpool The Beatles were his all-time favourite band "Do you know what Charlotte, all the pop groups over the years must have had children and none have made a record with those lyrics I reckon that's a number 1 hit, what do you think my darling" his wife Kate looked at him with that familiar look every husband knows "Yes dear, definitely maybe the b side could be, Not Long Now" Charlie started to laugh "mummy being funny but I like it, right campers we shall just park here in this little car park to stretch our legs" the family exited the car and started to do stretching exercises Charlie was leaning on a dry stone wall which are dotted around the English Lake District and proudly announced "Right campers I'm going to show you a little piece of history you see that rock painted white" Charlotte and Kate were looking at where Charlie was pointing "Oh yes is that the one that fell out of ETs spaceship darling" Kate was teasing Charlie. "Very good mummy, no, no that piece of rock is called the Bishop of Barf. The story goes Lord

Bassenthwaite who was the lord of the manor around these parts many years ago, had a race with one of his guests on horseback to the Bishop of Barf. His guest was supposedly dressed in a knights suit of armour and legend has it that ever since that race the people of that pub have to paint the Bishop of Barf white, what do you think of that Charlotte? A mind of useless information me" Charlie was standing with a little grin on his face looking at Kate and Charlotte "gosh daddy, do you think it was King Arthur" said Charlotte "It could have been sweetheart who knows" suddenly Kate announced, "right I have a little surprise as well" Kate said grabbing hold of Charlie and Charlottes hand she said proudly "Now turn around and look up at that mountain with the rocks on the top now you have to be patient if you look carefully it looks like a lion and a lamb" the three of them were looking at the rocks from all different angles suddenly Charlie announced "Whoa your right darling it does can you see it Charlotte" "No I can't see it, oh yes I can, oh wait it's gone" "Now then Charlotte it is called an optical illusion" Kate was rather pleased with herself "now wasn't that better than that piece of rock Charlotte" Charlie looked at Kate in a mock sad expression "Darling you can be so crushing at times" said Charlie to Kate. "Aah di dums sweetheart, knight in armour indeed. Right, everybody are we all refreshed? off we go to Bassenthwaite Hall" Kate announced "Ok my lady off we go on our own magical mystery tour woohoo" Charlie was doing his little dance towards the car "Yes daddy and you can be the walrus" "Kate and Charlie were laughing at Charlotte referring to John Lennon's song "I am the walrus" "very good sweetheart."

The family were now driving up the long drive to Bassenthwaite Hall Charlotte suddenly cried out "daddy, daddy look a blue pheasant" Charlie and Kate were looking to where Charlotte was pointing "goodness me, well Charlotte this is your first sighting of a peacock I wonder will he spread his wings" Charlie stopped the car, as if on cue the peacock turned towards the car and opened his beautiful plumage it's body was a beautiful iridescent blue the crest on its head gave him a proud regal look its tail had turned into a beautiful fan shimmering in the sunlight a thousand eyes looking as if saying keep away "oh my goodness isn't he a beauty" Charlie was mesmerised by the image in front of him and then as if on cue again, the peacock tucked his tail away and gave a screeching cry and wandered off looking for food as if nothing happened. Kate placed her fingers in her ears and sighed "gosh he's very noisy isn't he." Kate was looking at Charlotte "yes but he looks like something out of a fairy tale mummy" Charlotte was still looking at the peacock "well I think that was a good sign we're going to have a wonderful time at

Bassenthwaite Hall and your ladyship, remember I told you I am a mind of useless information well, these old manor houses used peacocks to keep away foxes and would be intruders with that screeching noise it would be very effective, you see your married to a very clever husband" Charlie turned to Kate with that silly grin she knew so well Kate responded with a reply worthy of Oscar Wilde

"Says the man who doesn't know what day the bins go out" Kate was looking at Charlie with the look Charlie knew "malady can be so beastly at times but, let's be on our way"

The family were now parked outside Bassenthwaite Hall it was Charlie who got out of the car first "wow it looks bigger than what I thought it's very palatial isn't it" Charlie was impressed "I wonder if Jeeves will meet us" Charlie was referring to the name Jeeves which is always associated to an english butler he was getting in the spirit of things now "will malady be dining in the main hall tonight" said Charlie "malady will beat you about the head with her brolly if you don't be quite now let's get the cases, you're the butler today sweetheart" Kate was also getting into the holiday mood now "your right sweetheart you just can't get the staff nowadays, right Charlotte you can carry daddies case and I'll get mummies huge case with all her stuff in" Charlie was teasing Kate but she was having her own bit of fun "I've told you a million times, don't exaggerate" then Charlie and Kate stopped what they were doing "daddy, daddy quick I don't like it" Charlie quickly looked where Charlotte was, "coming sweetheart" he began walking towards Charlotte "look daddy those horrid little creatures on the wall" "Ha-ha there called gargoyles there made of stone" Charlie picked up Charlotte and began to explain "what happens when it rains water comes down those pipes and then gushes out of the gargoyles mouths very clever isn't it" daddy said "yes or weird" Kate piped up, Charlotte was still in her daddies arms when she shouted "look there here" Charlie and Kate looked where Charlotte was pointing up in the skies and there they where, a flight of swallows and a flock of house martins Charlie was excited and shouted "it truly is summer now just look at them, the Dolphins of the air, this is going to be a great holiday, Kate my love, make a note of the date" it was something they did every year they made a note on the calendar at home when the swallows and house martins arrived they knew summer was truly here"ok campers I'll book us in, and you two can have a wander around you never know, you might bump into Jeeves what a great weekend this is going to be" Charlie was walking to reception singing happily to himself.

Charlie met up with Kate and Charlotte after finishing the signing in formalities "Righty ho campers room 36, it's gets even better we've been upgraded, lake view and a mini suite" Charlie had a big grin on his face as he announced his news to Charlotte and Kate "Wow I'm impressed how did you manage that" "Well I've still got my powers of persuasion, right 2nd floor there's the lift"Charlie was walking towards the lift "Wait a minute lazy bones we will walk up, just look at that grand staircase, we will look like a Lord and Lady and Charlotte, you can be our little princess" Charlottes face lit up like a Christmas tree "Oh yes daddy let's walk up the stairs I want to be a princess" "Well how can I refuse that, come on then hold my hand" mum dad and Charlotte in the middle holding her mum and dads hand proceeded to walk up the stairs taking in the beautiful surroundings "Your quite right darling we shall walk up this grand staircase while our butler chappie is taking our bags to our suite we shall see if there's a drawing room where we can partake of afternoon tea and some lovely cream cakes" Charlie announced "A drawing room were not going to draw pictures are we I thought we were having cream cakes" said Charlotte.

"No no silly girl a drawing room is a room which these big manor houses have its actually called, a withdrawing room where you could leave the main room and chill out, I told you a mind of useless information me isn't that right sweetheart" Charlie said looking at Kate, a big grin on his face Kate said nothing the rolling of the eyes said it all.

"Wow look at this wooden panelling the craftsmanship is amazing" Charlie didn't know what to look at next "Just look at the stair spindles they look like big barley sugar sticks" Charlie was truly amazed at the workmanship "I know what a beautiful house" Kate was looking around her in awe of her surroundings the oil paintings of Lord and Lady Bassenthwaite then suddenly Charlotte shouted "Mummy Daddy look it's King Arthur" Charlie and Kate looked towards where Charlotte was pointing "Oh my goodness" Charlie literally stopped in his tracks open mouthed looking at the stain glass window that adorned the staircase landing the three of them just stood looking at it, as if in a trance because there in all his glory emblazoned on the stain glass window was a proud looking knight in his suit of armour his large hands resting on a gold handled sword, the knights golden locks his piercing eyes, his chiseled face which was adorned with a goatee beard demonstrated a man of great prowess a very serious look on his face, a white horse, in the background standing proud and majestic like its owner, and then out of nowhere a voice said "A splendid fellow is he not" the three of them suddenly snapped out of their reverie and turned towards the voice "He is Lord Bassenthwaite himself, Lord of the Manor which is Bassenthwaite Hall" the voice announced "He certainly is" said Charlie looking back towards the window "Of course there are people so it is said who think it isn't him at all" said the voice who was also looking at the window "Goodness me who else could it be" said Kate looking at their new friend "Well legend has it that it could be, Don Quixote" said the voice

"Don Quixote but he's a fictional character written by Cervantes and he lived in Spain, in La Mancha" said Charlie. "Oh indeed Don Quixote was a fictional character and senor Cervantes did write the tales of Don Quixote but, legend and urban myths intertwine over centuries but, don't you think he looks a little like him" their new friend was now looking at Charlie, who in turn was looking back at the window he was trying to think of pictures of Don Quixote he started talking aloud "Well he did have a goatee beard he certainly looks a very proud chap erm, Oh my gosh" Charlie almost fell over "Shush Charlie what on earths the matter"Said Kate "The knight he just, he, he just winked at me I swear he winked at me" Charlie was trying to compose himself "Ha-ha you have witnessed the little phenomenon" said the stranger "You mean it's a trick of some sort" Charlie feeling slightly embarrassed "Well over the years people have said that he has winked at them, I can only assume it is a trick of the light the way it shines on the stain glass they do say Lord Bassenthwaite was a bit of a character maybe he instructed the glass maker to do it who knows indeed, Don Quixote himself shall we say, was a little eccentric" said the voice "Well I don't know it's certainly a work of art in itself" said Charlie looking back at the window "Indeed it is, well I must be getting back to work time waits for no one, I have put your bags in your room just ring reception if you need anything" the stranger was about to walk down the stairs then suddenly stopped and turned back and announced, "My name is Jeeves by the way have a lovely stay" and he proceeded to walk down the stairs Charlie could only stand open mouthed looking at Jeeves walking away it was Kate who broke the silence "Close your mouth sweetheart, you look like your catching flies" said Kate who was now in fits of laughter "Is he having a laugh Jeeves, his name is Jeeves, goodness me let's see what our room is like you never know Justin Beiber might be on the balcony singing, "Charlotte Charlotte were for art thou Charlotte" Charlie was referring to the famous love story Romeo and Juliet and Justin Beiber was one of the families favourite singers, the family we're now entering their room.

"Woohoo look at this room, it's brilliant" Charlie couldn't contain himself Kate jumped on the four poster bed

"Oh this is heaven, lovely and soft jump up Charlotte what do you think" Charlotte hadn't stopped smiling since she walked through the door. "It really is like Downton Abbey mummy, I've never seen a bed with a roof before" Charlotte was still amazed by it all.

"that's called a four poster bed sweetheart" Charlotte was entering the bathroom "wow look daddy we have a bathroom as well" "that's right sweetheart it's called a ensuite" Charlie was now walking towards the bay window "Will you look at this view goodness me" the family were now looking out of the window at the shimmering lake the beautiful flowers in full bloom, house martins and swallows flying through the air catching insects on the wing "Isn't this just wonderful we are going to have a lovely weekend" suddenly Charlie started doing his little dance Charlotte and Kate were used to his little ways and were laughing

"Do you know what I reckon" said Charlie unpacking his case "I think our friend Jeeves has his little tale down to a fine art he must wait till people walk up the stairs they then look up at the window and then, Jeeves appears as if from nowhere , No I think old Jeeveesie has a bit of a sense of humour what do you think darling" he asked Kate "Well how do you explain the knight winking at you" Kate was teasing Charlie now "Well as he said a trick of the light but, he certainly looked like Don Quixote the little goatee beard, dressed as a knight, no no listen to me what am I like I'm getting carried away, a fictional Spanish knight hobnobbing it with Lord Bassenthwaite in England no no anyway let's get ourselves sorted and have a wander around"

Having settled in and showered and changed into fresh clothes the family were now having their evening meal in the restaurant in Bassenthwaite Hall "Well that was a grand dinner" announced Charlie "you can't beat a good sticky toffee pudding is madam struggling with hers I could always assist" Charlie looked at Kate with that silly look which she knew well "No no madam is quite fine thank you I'm taking my time, not like you greedy guts, Charlotte don't you love ice cream and sticky toffee pudding on the spoon together just running into one another hmm lovely" Kate was enjoying her dessert and of course teasing Charlie, Charlotte suddenly piped up "Daddy I thought you were on a diet" "I am sweetheart it's called a seafood diet see food and eat it haha."

The family were now in there room getting ready for bed the day had taken its toll and they were all very tired "Right sweetheart let's get you tucked in ready for a lovely day tomorrow" Charlie ruffled Charlottes hair and gave her a kiss on the forehead Kate then sat on the bed gave her a goodnight kiss then said "Did you have a good day today Charlotte" "Yes I thought the knight in the window was really cool, daddy" Charlotte a mischievous little smile on her face "Night knight Daddy" she had been waiting to say that all night after mummy explained it to her "I'll do the jokes sweetheart nitey nite" Charlotte rolled over onto the big pillow a big smile on her face she remembered something "Daddy can you put my favourite record on to get me asleep" "Of course sweetheart" Charlie picked up his iPhone and selected Spotify and selected Charlottes favourite song by Ariana Grande she closed her eyes and images from the day flashed through her head while Ariana sang her song, the drive up the motorway stopping at the service station feeding the ducks outside the cafe, then arriving at the hotel it really is like Downton Abbey and the window, with the knight, I wonder if he really was one of King Arthurs knights of the round table, Charlotte was deep in her thoughts as sleep was taking over as Ariana Grande sang the last of her song her voice trailing away as sleep took over.

Taptaptap a noise on the window made Charlotte stir in her sleep taptaptap that noise again "Daddy is that you" Charlotte was half asleep rubbing her eyes sitting up in her bed she looked over to her mum and dad who were asleep taptaptap the noise is coming from the window she thought, Charlotte got out of bed and walked towards the window she pulled the curtains apart and there sitting on a horse was the knight from the window he was talking but she couldn't hear him he was pointing at the window handle, she opened the window slightly "Charlotte it is I Don Quixote and may I introduce you to my trusty steed foxy lady" the knight just sat there on his horse smiling, it was foxy lady who Charlotte goes to see every Saturday at the nearby farm where they live but how can this be "Oh my gosh" Charlotte brought her hands to her mouth "Oh my gosh, foxy lady has wings and she has changed into a unicorn what does this mean" Don Quixote started to speak again "Quick Charlotte put this around you" he passed Charlotte a cape through the window she took the cape from him it was a lovely emerald green cape with a hood, she placed it around her pulling the hood up she caught sight of herself in the mirror suddenly the cape was shimmering with twinkling lights which looked like tiny diamonds   suddenly young Charlotte was looking at her older self. Quick as a flash it was young Charlotte again. "Quick Charlotte, we have plenty to see and so little time to see it" Don Quixote was holding out his hand "Trust me Charlotte, I am a noble knight I will look after you" Charlotte held out her hand before she knew it she was sitting on foxy lady flying through the air "Don Quixote I'm scared where are we going" "Don't be scared Charlotte my name is Don Quixote am a chivalrous knight of honour and, a time traveller"Don Quixote gestured with his arm and bowed his head "Gosh you mean like Dr

Who"said Charlotte "I know not of this doctor fellow" Charlotte didn't answer she couldn't keep her eyes off foxy lady or more to the point the golden horn on her head and the beautiful white wings they seemed to whisper to her as they flew through the air the clouds seemed like marshmallows, she felt as if she could walk on them she was trying to think of the bedtime story her daddy told her about a flying horse from Greek mythology "Pegasus" Don Quixote shouted out "His name is Pegasus Charlotte" Said Don Quixote "But how did you know I was thinking about that" "No matter Charlotte we have a lion to see" "A lion, in England, don't be silly" "Whoa foxy lady, there Charlotte you see our proud friend" and there on top of the mountain was a lion roaring at them a lamb standing meekly beside him "but Mummy said it was an illusion" "Indeed Charlotte, don't believe everything you see" Charlotte was looking at Don Quixote then back at the lion but all she was looking at was a clump of rocks "Quick Charlotte wrap your cloak around you tell me, have you ever heard a bell ring underwater" "No I haven't it wouldn't work silly" "Well hold tight Charlotte off we go" Suddenly Don Quixote burst into song, it sounded very familiar to Charlotte yes, that's it, *funiculi funicula* a famous Italian song mummy plays when she's having a bath then Charlotte suddenly joined Don Quixote in singing it "Charlotte your familiar with the great man" "Yes it's my mummies favourite song Ravioli I think his name is" "Ha-ha you joke with me, Ravioli indeed, he is the colossus of the opera world Pavarotti his name is, tell me Charlotte who is your favourite tenor" "Well I quite like Justin Bieber and I like Rag and Bone Man but my favourite is Ariana Grande she is so cool" "Rag and Bone indeed, I think you joke with Don Quixote" Suddenly Don Quixote became serious "Quite now Charlotte we are here, steady foxy lady we must wait, and listen" Don Quixote was cupping his hand to his ear "What are we listening for" whispered Charlotte "Tell me Charlotte when is a lake not a lake" said Don Quixote "I know this one when it is frozen" said Charlotte looking very pleased with herself with a wave of his hand Don Quixote said "no Charlotte when it is a village" and there in the light of the full moon was indeed a village she looked again at him once more confused than Don Quixote announced "The beautiful village of Mardale Charlotte, it was flooded many years ago to make a reservoir and some say, they can hear the church bells of the Holy Trinity church listen, can you hear them" Charlotte was listening suddenly she said "yes I can do you think someone is getting married?" she turned to look at Don Quixote "maybe and look, can you see the weather vane on top of the church a lamb, and a sword, have you not noticed the great and modest Don Quixote does not have a sword" Charlotte looked at the weather vane then at Don Quixote and indeed, his sword was missing "That can't be yours, how can that be" Charlotte was looking at Don Quixote "it is indeed I was on a time travelling journey like now I came upon a gentleman wandering lonely as an oak tree then all at once" Charlotte suddenly cut him off "erm don't you mean clouds" Charlotte said "William Wordsworth was a brilliant man but not a man to take advice clouds indeed, but quick Charlotte we must be on our way and leave Excalibur for another day"

"Excalibur" Charlotte said open mouthed "you mean King Arthurs sword" Charlotte couldn't say anything else she just looked in total awe at Don Quixote who announced in a sad voice "alas Charlotte when King Arthur was mortally wounded in battle, he was taken to the magical isle of Avalon where Merlin himself, entrusted me to look after Excalibur and that's where it sits until a knight in shining armour is entrusted to carry on King Arthurs odyssey but enough of this chit chat we must be on our way, off we go Foxy Lady." "but what will happen to your sword when the water returns" "fear not Charlotte I told you, I am a time traveller what you are seeing is what happened nearly a hundred years ago Excalibur now sits atop the church in the next village called Shap but quick, wrap your cloak around you off we go on are next adventure, off we go"our three adventurers arrived at there next destination when Don Quixote announced

"Tell me Charlotte, when is a bird not a bird" Don Quixote was enjoying himself now "oh I know this one, when it's a liver bird ha-ha I win" Charlotte was referring to the famous mythical birds that sit atop of the liver buildings in Liverpool where she went on a school trip and seen them up close they were huge "No when it is a Bluebird"they were now over Coniston Water the famous lake were Sir Donald Campbell sadly died while attempting a water speed record in 1967 Don Quixote pointed to the lake which was covered in an ethereal mist then suddenly out of the mist came the famous Bluebird "Don Quixote what is it" Charlotte couldn't work out what to think of this beautiful machine it was as if it was flying over the lake she looked wide eyed in awe of what she was looking at "Charlotte I'm not familiar with your modern words but to me, it is a beautiful water chariot it could have been created by Michelangelo himself, but quickly Charlotte let us wave goodbye to a truly honourable knight who navigates the Bluebird for all eternity" they were both waving in the direction of the Bluebird, Charlotte thought the man was waving back but in an instant the Bluebird disappeared and the shimmering mist flooded over the lake again.

"Hold tight Charlotte we now go to a truly magical place, hold tight" They were now back flying through the clouds Charlotte still couldn't believe what was happening "Now

Charlotte we are here, steady foxy lady, tell me when is a circle, not a circle"Don Quixote was enjoying himself now, teasing Charlotte with his riddles "I definitely know this one, when it is a squircle" Charlotte knew this because Charlie had used the name in a game of scrabble, Kate thought he was cheating but he was proved right he even got a double word score which didn't please Kate "No Don Quixote wins again when it's a stone circle, this place Charlotte, is truly a magical place look" Don Quixote was pointing down to the stone circle "This place Charlotte is called Castle Rigg, I was last here when the Romans were here and it was old then so goodness knows how old it is" "The Romans you mean, the Romans who had Gladiators, but that was a thousand years ago your pulling my leg" Charlotte was still looking at the stone circle "Don Quixote pulls no one's leg you talk gibberish" Charlotte was looking down at the stone circle the people looked like ants but as they got nearer she could make out the people now, she suddenly spoke out loud "Gosh they really our Roman soldiers" Charlotte was looking spellbound at the site below "Charlotte let me tell you about this place, this was a trading place where people from different continents traded their wares they travelled on what was called ley lines your modern words you would call Motorways the ley lines would connect with other stone circles which would act as trading points the main one being Stonehenge and then beyond your shores they would lead to the greatest ley line of all the great Silk Road leading to what you now call China a truly vast and mysterious country have you ever been to China Charlotte" Don Quixote looked at Charlotte waiting for an answer. "Well I have been to the China garden with mummy and daddy, I like the fortune cookies at the end of your meal" Don Quixote looked at Charlotte with a puzzled look on his face "I know not of the China garden or fortune cookies I told you, you talk gibberish sometimes"

"Don Quixote can I ask you a question" Charlotte was looking at Don Quixote with a curious look "of course Charlotte ask me anything" "Well, don't you get lonely travelling around, don't you have any family" she was looking at him in a kind of sad way she waited for his reply which duly came in a typical Don Quixote way, "how can Don Quixote be lonely Charlotte, I can always travel back in time to see my great friends like Charles Dickens I had great expectations for Charles ha-ha or, my other great friend John Lennon suddenly Don Quixote burst into song "Apple pie and custard forever" Charlotte started laughing "don't you mean strawberry fields forever that's my daddies favourite song" Charlotte was still laughing "Pah, John could be so stubborn at times" "well Imagine that" Charlotte was grinning at her own little joke "it is almost sunrise Charlotte, tell me have you ever sat on a rainbow" Don Quixote was enjoying himself now because he knew the magical vision that Charlotte was about to see would stay with her for the rest of her life"Don't be silly no I haven't sat on a rainbow, oh my gosh" Charlotte was looking open mouthed at the beautiful sight in front of her it was a double rainbow she had never seen one before it was twinkling as if it was moving "Don Quixote how is this possible" she couldn't take her eyes off the spectacle in front of her "Charlotte hold tight prepare yourself to see the most magical images of you life, steady foxy lady" they now seemed to float towards the rainbow "Charlotte hold my hand I will show you what people only see in their dreams" the two of them seemed to be floating towards the ark of the rainbow they left foxy lady standing on a white cloud her white wings outstretched her golden horn acting like a beacon towards the rainbow "Tell me Charlotte how does it feel to sit where no other person has sat, to sit with Iris herself the goddess of rainbows, a rainbow Charlotte is the ladder between the heavens and the earth" "gosh do you mean like the internet, my friend at school is called Iris" Charlotte was looking at Don Quixote waiting for a reply "I told you Charlotte I know not of your modern words but, your friend is a lucky girl being named after such a beautiful goddess but, let us hurry we are near the end of your magical adventure this is your beautiful world it truly is a wonderful world" Charlotte sat transfixed unable to comprehend the sights in front of her "Look" Don Quixote was pointing towards a clump of clouds that were slowly disappearing "Oh my gosh it's the Eiffel Tower how is that possible and there, it's the Sydney opera house we went there last year to see a pop concert and daddy climbed the Sydney Harbour Bridge, oh my gosh there's Sydney harbour bridge but how is this possible" Charlotte just sat looking open mouthed at the dreamscape in front of her she turned to look at Don Quixote for an answer she was tongue tied no words would come "These are but some of the places you will see in your lifetime Charlotte, we have not finished yet look" Don Quixote was pointing to a cloud which was slowly disappearing "oh my gosh is that the Empire State Building how is this possible it's like I'm dreaming" Charlotte just sat looking at the images in front of her in total awe she was distracted by a cloud emitting lightning bolts which was slowly disappearing to reveal Big Ben the clock on the Houses of Parliament in London she just sat transfixed, at the bottom of the clock there were people milling about going about their everyday business to wherever they were going Charlotte noticed people sitting outside a cafe obviously having lunch she suddenly looked at one particular lady and cried "That's me, that's the lady in the mirror, when I tried the cloak on, Don Quixote am I dreaming" she said waiting for an answer "Well maybe you are dreaming Charlotte but it could be you, when we next meet again we will sit on this rainbow, foxy lady will fly us through the heavens up to the rings of Saturn, we will then shake hands with your favourite star constellation Orion himself" Charlotte sat looking ahead then back to Don Quixote unable to take in this dream like time in her life finally, she managed to speak "Don" that's all she could say she still couldn't take her eyes away from the dreamlike images in front of her "Charlotte take one last look we must go the sun is rising, off we go" quick as a flash they were back on foxy lady the clouds rushing past them like cotton balls flying through the air Charlotte was unable to take in the surroundings everything was a blur.

"Goodbye Charlotte until we meet again if I don't see you soon, I shall see you through the window ha-ha and Charlotte don't worry about those pesky exams everything will be ok, goodbye" then suddenly foxy lady reared up on her hind legs flapped her wings as if to say goodbye and then the noble knight and his beautiful winged horse where gone.

"Charlotte wakey wakey time to get up sweetheart come along lazy bones" Charlottes dad was teasing her "Don Quixote come back I want to sit on the rainbow" Charlotte was half asleep and half awake "Do you indeed well he can take me with you as well" Charlottes dad was sitting on her bed ruffling her hair Kate was also now sitting on Charlottes bed "now then you sound as if you had a lovely dream sweetheart sitting on a rainbow wow." "But daddy, mummy he was here I did sit on a rainbow we saw the Eiffel Tower and Sydney opera house even the Empire State Building" Charlotte couldn't stop talking "Come along sweetie pie let's get you showered then we can go down for breakfast and you can tell us all about your lovely dream" Charlotte was now sitting up in her bed "But daddy it wasn't a dream he was here the knight in the window his name is Don Quixote we flew through the air on foxy lady but she was a unicorn and she had wings" "Goodness me foxy lady as well, ok you just have a lovely warm shower and get all that stardust off you". Kate was walking Charlotte towards the bathroom "Hello, where did this come from" Kate picked up the green cloak what had kept Charlotte warm in her dream "Don Quixote gave it to me to keep warm while we flew through the air mummy, it really happened we seen Roman soldiers and a bluebird that looked like a car on water" Charlotte couldn't stop talking about her adventure "Ok sweetheart let's get you showered and you can tell us all about it over breakfast."

Charlotte her mum and dad where now walking down the stairs on their way to breakfast suddenly as if on cue they stopped and looked up at the knight in the window.

Charlotte broke the silence "Mummy, daddy do you think it was just a dream?" Charlottes mum and dad both looked at each other then looked at Charlotte her face as long as a wet weekend "Who knows sweetheart it was lucky Don Quixote was passing this way" All three then turned towards the window as if as one, they all gasped "He's done it again!" it was Charlie this time who broke the silence. Charlotte suddenly cried out "It was real he said, I'll see you through the window" her laughter filled the cavernous stairwell. Charlie and Kate did not have the heart to tell Charlotte it was another trick of the light but they both looked at each other as if to say was it real? "Next time Charlotte ask your knight chappie if mum and dad can come along. Shall we have our breakfast and you can tell us all about your wonderful adventure"

All three where now walking down the stairs when they reached the bottom Charlotte couldn't resist taking one last look "Goodbye proud knight I'll see you in my dreams" she whispered, she waved goodbye all three of them then walked towards the dining room then suddenly without warning Jeeves the butler appeared "Good morning sir, I've made a table up for you in the conservatory you have a lovely view of the lake. I believe you like smoked kipper's sir?" asked Jeeves.Smoked kippers are an English breakfast dish which consists of the herring fish which is smoked then grilled "Indeed I do you can't beat a smoked kipper on sourdough toast soaked in butter topped with a poached egg and gently brushed with Dijon mustard" Charlie was looking at Jeeves with a little smile on his face Jeeves looked at Charlie with a deadpan face and announced "well I'm afraid we've no smoked kippers left sir, can I show you to your table madam" "Eh, oh thank you." Jeeves proceeded to show Charlotte and Kate to their table Charlie following behind whilst thinking to himself how did he know I liked kippers. Just as Charlie was about to sit down, he noticed Kate with her head in her hands she couldn't contain her laughter anymore "oh dear me the look on your face when Jeeves said there were no kippers available today your face looked like it had been slapped with a wet kipper, never mind a smoked one". Charlie sat down looked at Kate who still had the giggles looked at Charlotte and said "well I think I will have a lovely bowl of creamy porridge". Jeeves appeared from nowhere and announced "will that be brushed with honey sir?" Charlie could only mutter "oh yes thank you" which once again sent Kate off into a giggling fit.

The family tucked into their breakfast and just as they had all finished Charlotte suddenly whispered to Charlie "daddy your friend is coming over" Jeeves asked the family "is everyone finished can I take your plates away" Charlie responded "You certainly can. That was a grand breakfast it will keep us going till we get to our next destination which is Castle Rigg Are you familiar with Castle Rigg Jeeves? I am told it is over a thousand years old" Before Jeeves could answer Charlotte piped up "yes daddy it is it leads to Stonehenge by ley lines the Romans used to trade there" "gosh Charlotte where did you learn that" Charlie sat open mouthed he looked at Kate who shrugged as if to say I haven't a clue. Jeeves broke the silence "the young lady is correct, according to historians stone circles were indeed trading markets that led to each other by ley lines indeed the biggest ley line was" Charlotte interrupted Jeeves again and blurted out "the silk road" Charlie, Kate and Jeeves could only look at Charlotte in amazement. Jeeves once again broke the silence and slowly said "déjà vu, I believe" he was referring to the strange feeling you have been somewhere before. "well I don't know what it is, we best be on our way to Castle Rigg, as time waits for no one". Charlie stood up and looked at Kate surprised and said "why did I say time waits for no one" "I don't know darling but it has been a funny old start to the day come along Charlotte let's be on our way goodbye Jeeves and thank you for a wonderful stay" said Kate. "Yes thank you Jeeves it has certainly been different". Jeeves shook Charlie by the hand and said "well sir until we meet again, please take this as a reminder of your stay" it was a key ring which Jeeves placed in Charlie's shirt pocket. The family where making their way out of the breakfast room when Charlotte suddenly said "can we say goodbye to our knight in the window?" "Yes of course sweetheart" Charlie, Kate and Charlotte stood at the bottom of the stairs "Goodbye noble knight until we meet again, maybe?" Charlotte suddenly remembered something "daddy what did Jeeves give you" Charlie put his hand in his shirt pocket and passed the key ring to Charlotte it was a piece of leather with a coin like piece of metal on it, one side was a knights head and she turned it over and got a pleasant shock because there on the key ring was the winged unicorn rearing up as if ready to fly "it really did happen" Charlotte face broke into a big smile she held on to Charlie and Kate's hands as they walked to the door and suddenly, they caught sight of Jeeves who was waving goodbye to them and then did something extraordinary, Jeeves raised his finger to his lips and gave them a wink. Charlie just stood open mouthed it was Charlotte who broke the silence "come along daddy time waits for no one" and then she started singing *funiculi funicula* as she skipped her way to the car. Charlie and Kate followed her then hugged each other and laughed "this is certainly going to be a night to remember!"

THE END………or is it?

www.ingramcontent.com/pod-product-compliance
Lightning Source LLC
Chambersburg PA
CBHW070455170726
48291CB00005B/1764